HELPING YOUR BRAND-NEW READER

Here's how to make first-time reading easy and fun:

▶ Read the introduction at the beginning of the book aloud. Look through the pictures together so that your child can see what happens in the story before reading the words.

▶ Read one or two pages to your child, placing your finger under each word.

▶ Let your child touch the words and read the rest of the story. Give him or her time to figure out each new word.

▶ If your child gets stuck on a word, you might say, *"Try something. Look at the picture. What would make sense?"*

▶ If your child is still stuck, supply the right word. This will allow him or her to continue to read and enjoy the story. You might say, *"Could this word be 'ball'?"*

▶ Always praise your child. Praise what he or she reads correctly, and praise good tries too.

▶ Give your child lots of chances to read the story again and again. The more your child reads, the more confident he or she will become.

▶ Have fun!

First edition 2006

Library of Congress Cataloging-in-Publication Data is available.

Library of Congress Catalog Card Number 2006042573

ISBN-13: 978-0-7636-2723-2
ISBN-10: 0-7636-2723-2

2 4 6 8 10 9 7 5 3 1

Printed in China

This book was typeset in Letraset Arta.
The illustrations were done in watercolor, marker, and colored pencil.

Candlewick Press
2067 Massachusetts Avenue
Cambridge, Massachusetts 02140

visit us at www.candlewick.com

LUCY
AND
BOB

CANDLEWICK PRESS
CAMBRIDGE, MASSACHUSETTS

written and illustrated by
David Martin

Contents

LOOK AT ME FLY

Introduction

This story is called *Look at Me Fly*. It's about how Lucy and Bob watch butterflies. First one butterfly is flying. Then two butterflies are flying, and then more and more — until *one hundred* butterflies are flying. Then Lucy wants to fly too!

One butterfly is flying.

4

Two butterflies are flying.

Three butterflies are flying.

Four butterflies are flying.

Five butterflies are flying.

One hundred butterflies are flying.

9

"Look at me fly," says Lucy.

10

"Look at me fly!"

HOPPING UP AND DOWN

Introduction

This story is called *Hopping Up and Down*. It's about how Bob hops up and lands on a rock, then hops down and lands on the grass. Then Lucy does *almost* the same thing.

Bob hops up.

Bob lands on the rock.

Bob hops down.

16

Bob lands on the grass.

Lucy hops up.

Lucy lands on the rock.

Lucy hops down.

20

Lucy lands on Bob.

FLIES FOR LUNCH

21

Introduction

This story is called *Flies for Lunch.* It's about how Bob sees a fly and—*Zap!*—catches it. Then Lucy sees a fly and—*Zap!*—catches it. But when Bob and Lucy see another fly, they *do not* catch it.

Bob sees a fly.

24

Zap! He catches it.

25

Lucy sees a fly.

26

Zap! She catches it.

27

Bob and Lucy see another fly.

Bob and Lucy smile.

Zap!

30

Bob and Lucy do not catch the fly.

TAG, YOU'RE IT!

Introduction

This story is called *Tag, You're It!* It's about how Bob and Lucy play tag. First Bob tags Lucy and says, "Tag, you're it!" Then they take turns chasing and tagging each other. Finally Lucy chases Bob underwater, but when she says "Tag, you're it!" it sounds like *"Blub, blub blub!"*

"Tag, you're it!" says Bob.

Lucy chases Bob.

"Tag, you're it!" says Lucy.

Bob chases Lucy.

"Tag, you're it!" says Bob.

38

Lucy chases Bob.

Lucy chases Bob underwater.

"Blub, blub blub!" says Lucy.